DON'T RUSH TO GET OLD

OLIVIA JACKSON

authorHOUSE

AuthorHouse™
1663 Liberty Drive
Bloomington, IN 47403
www.authorhouse.com
Phone: 1 (800) 839-8640

© 2016 Olivia Jackson. All rights reserved.

No part of this book may be reproduced, stored in a retrieval system, or transmitted by any means without the written permission of the author.

Published by AuthorHouse   06/25/2016

ISBN: 978-1-5246-0005-1 (sc)
ISBN: 978-1-5049-8710-3 (hc)
ISBN: 978-1-5246-0004-4 (e)

Library of Congress Control Number: 2016904888

Print information available on the last page.

Any people depicted in stock imagery provided by Thinkstock are models, and such images are being used for illustrative purposes only.
Certain stock imagery © Thinkstock.

This book is printed on acid-free paper.

Because of the dynamic nature of the Internet, any web addresses or links contained in this book may have changed since publication and may no longer be valid. The views expressed in this work are solely those of the author and do not necessarily reflect the views of the publisher, and the publisher hereby disclaims any responsibility for them.

KJV
Scripture quotations marked KJV are from the Holy Bible, King James Version (Authorized Version). First published in 1611. Quoted from the KJV Classic Reference Bible, Copyright © 1983 by The Zondervan Corporation.

FOREWORD

Olivia's story is an incredible testimony of God's goodness. She refused to allow the challenges of her past to negatively impact her present, and ultimately her future. The power of her testimony is unveiled in this book which provides insight to young women and girls to embrace where they are on the way to where they are going.

All too often young girls find themselves in a race to grow up, that is, until they are met with adult responsibilities that rob them of their youth. Although no one is immune to the trials that life may bring, we all have the power to choose how we allow these trials to influence us. Olivia found victory over her trials when she learned to cast her cares on Jesus; and she also garnered the courage to motivate others.

Olivia has developed into a great wife, mother, and a well-rounded woman who is learning to balance and prioritize the blessings that God has provided. When Olivia allowed God to transform the trials in her life into triumphs, it added grace, favor, and a testimony that is certain to encourage others to overcome similar obstacles. "They overcame him by the blood of the Lamb and by the word of their testimony..." ~ (Revelation 12:11 NIV) I have been privileged to know Olivia for several years. She is an active member of Christian Faith Fellowship Church, the church I pastor (with my husband) in Milwaukee, Wisconsin. I am confident this book will change the lives of many, and I am eager to see what more God has in store for Olivia's life.

~Leah Williams
Pastor, Author, Entrepreneur

TABLE OF CONTENTS

Chapter One – Special In The World 1

Chapter Two – In The Darkest Place 7

Chapter Three – Picture Perfect Turnaround 17

Chapter Four – Lucky 11 29

Chapter Five – "Abreast" Of The Change 39

Chapter Six – The Immaculate Deception 47

Chapter Seven – Turned Out 55

Chapter Eight – Dancing With Death 65

Chapter Nine – Alive But Not Living 73

Chapter Ten – I Am… In The Building 81

Chapter Eleven – Angels On Television 87

Chapter Twelve – Life After The Rush 93

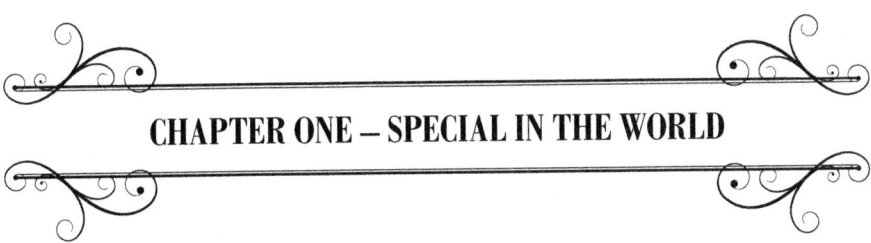

CHAPTER ONE – SPECIAL IN THE WORLD

"Our Father which are in heaven, hallowed be thy name. Thy Kingdom come, thy will be done on earth as it is in heaven. Give us this day our daily bread, and forgive us of our trespasses as we forgive those who have trespassed against us, lead us not into temptation but deliver us from evil, for thine is the Kingdom, the power and the glory forever…Amen - Matthew 6:9-12

It is the winter of 1975 in Milwaukee, WI. I am two years old and I am reciting this prayer in its entirety. I know this prayer like I know my own name, Olivia Jackson. My mother would always tell me how special I was to God because she earnestly prayed for a daughter. She believed that God heard her, and that He answered her prayer by sending me to her. She would say this prayer with us every night before we went to sleep. There was my older brother, who was 2 years older than I, and my younger brother, who was just a baby at the time. My mother was really big and adamant on prayer. Although she read the Bible to us as a method of getting to know God, she never took us to church. My mother did not believe that going to church was something that you had to do in order to know God. I beg to differ. You see, my mother grew up in a household where she was forced to go to church all the time. As soon as she became of age, she never went back to church again.

My mother had her first child, my brother, at the age of seventeen. As prevalent as teenage pregnancy is today, it is almost unbelievable to think that it was unacceptable and highly frowned upon "back in the day." This was ESPECIALLY true if you were unmarried and living in the South. In fact, it was almost considered taboo. This was particularly hard for my mom, who was the product of a religiously strict household. She eventually married at the age of 19 and then, off she went. The young mother and blushing bride literally ran away with her husband, leaving behind her entire family; migrating from West Memphis Tennessee to Benton Harbor Michigan… and that's where I came in.

According to my mom, she and my dad often talked about bringing a little girl into their family. Both my mom and my dad grew up in the church so they knew the way to get the baby girl they wanted was to petition God in prayer. The Bible clearly says, "Be anxious for nothing, but in everything by prayer and supplication, with thanksgiving, let your requests be made known to God" Philippians 4:6. So they prayed to God, on their knees together, and rendered a special prayer; asking Him to bless them with a little girl one night. Since my mom had a son from a previous relationship, a daughter would have certainly made their family complete. She said the night after their prayers was sent to heaven she became pregnant soon after. In her heart of hearts, mom knew, she just KNEW that she was expecting a girl! Sure enough, nine months later, July 29, 1972 guess who arrived? You guessed it, me! My mom would say that I entered the world as a smiling, cocoa skinned bundle of joy. My pleasant disposition seemed to express "I was happy to have arrived." Little did I know that soon I would be chartering a rocky and tumultuous journey called life… and it would give me very little to smile about.

There are certain things that happen to us when we are children. There are things that we learn and experience during those beginning years that our young minds may not be able to comprehend. Children are naturally inquisitive and as a result, they will ask anyone (specifically adults) to pacify their curiosity. As we get older, the answers, stories and reasoning that they give us are usually so astounding, that they are almost unbelievable and too good to be true. Who are the first people we turn to for confirmation? That's right, our parents, mommy and daddy. They are always there for us. For me, that assurance is a constant reminder of how God, the Father is to us, His children. We can trust in His word for our life because we know that He is our creator and He always has our best interests at heart. "Sovereign LORD, you are

God! Your covenant is trustworthy, and you have promised these good things to your servant." – 2 Samuel 7:28

In this regard (if parenting is done correctly), I think it is pertinent for children to see God's love in their parents first. After all, mom and dad are (or should be) their first example of God's love and His statutes. I feel that it is so important for children to realize that right or wrong, information received from mom or dad should be considered sincere; because like God, parents have (or should have) their child's best interests at heart. From infancy to adulthood, parents hold a special place of remembrance in their children's hearts.

For instance, my mom would share one particular story of me as a small child, barely walking. Stealthily, I managed to climb out of the bed where I slept with my parents and crawled downstairs to the kitchen. Somehow I reached up on the counter top just enough to grab the glass pitcher, which was sitting on the edge. Impulsively, I pulled it down on top of myself. The glass broke swiftly and cut me under my chin, gashing me from ear to ear. When my mother awakened in the middle of the night to find me missing from the bed; she said that a sheer panic had come over her. After she awakened my dad, they frantically began running from room to room looking for me. After searching all of the rooms upstairs, she went downstairs to find me sitting in the middle of the kitchen floor. I was sitting in a puddle of blood, laughing and playing as if nothing was wrong. She would always say that I was sent by God which made me very special in the earth. I was a pleasant and "good" baby who rarely cried. Instead of crying, I smiled, laughed and talked all the time. To her surprise I was seriously injured. Yet, no one could ever tell that by looking at me.

Recalling that story, I am reminded by a popular saying that "church folks" say. "I am so glad that I don't look like what I've been through." I would not truly understand or appreciate the true meaning of that declaration until years later.

Every time my mom would tell that story, I would think to myself, wow! God must really love me, because even though I was seriously injured and needed stitches from ear to ear, my mom said that I never missed a beat. Once I knew and understood who Satan was, and what he stood for, I always knew the devil was out to get me and in retrospect; this was his first attempt. You see, Satan's only initiative for human existence is to kill, steal and destroy. – John 10:10. The funny thing is that even if you try your best to live a holy and sanctified life, free from the proclivities of sin, the devil will NEVER cease from his "attempt to implement" his vicious plan of attack on our lives.

Throughout this book you will read about the many times Satan has crossed my path. I was truly engrossed in his work, and he was the center of most of my pain. You will also notice that some of the trauma that I experienced was truly designed to kill, steal and destroy my destiny…

BUT GOD!

As I reflect on this disheveled flashback, I shudder to think about how so many people are in this same predicament today. There are people who willingly commit themselves to unhealthy relationships, under the misconception that jealousy is a healthy component of love. I have witnessed, first-hand, the harmful effects of jealously in relationships, and let me tell you, jealousy in its selfish form does not embody the spirit of love. One of the greatest attributes of love is its ability to grow. If a person's mate, spouse, partner etc. keeps them from growing to be their absolute personal best because of jealousy, please understand and know beloved that person does not and cannot love them. "Love is patient, love is kind and is not jealous; love does not brag and is not arrogant;" – 1 Corinthians 13:4. Love can certainly throw you for a loop; it would if you are not ready.

It is funny how the brain functions. Without going into all of the biological details, the brain simply retains what it wants to – which is either voluntary or involuntary. This is especially true when it comes to recalling childhood memories. Unlike most adults, I do not remember my kindergarten teacher's name, my favorite class in middle school, or even my high school associates. I have a gap in my memory that omits most of my childhood and teenage years, and I am sure that the cause of the gap is because of some of the very traumatic events that have happened in my life. I am positive that God blocked those memories from existing because the pain would have truly paralyzed me from receiving

His will and direction for my life, and living in His "light." I would have merely existed, and those memories would have made me a permanent recipient and resident of darkness.

Although the memories I have are scarce, I can vividly recall an event that I will never forget. The weird thing is that some adults recall their earliest memories of the past at ages five and maybe even four years old. But this occurrence happened when I was two years old. The year is 1974. My family lived in Benton Harbor Michigan. I am doing what little girls do, playing tea party all by myself, when I heard the sound of laughter echoing from the hallway leading downstairs to where I was. The laughter was obviously female, but it was unfamiliar to me. I never heard the sound of that voice before, so I stopped playing to listen in closer. I could hear my dad's voice whispering. I could not decipher what he was saying, but it was blatantly clear that the woman he was whispering to was not my mother.

Quickly, I ran into the guest bedroom and pretended to be asleep, so I could listen and see who that woman was with my dad; and what they were doing downstairs in the house. I lied on the bed as still as a bump on a log, eyes tightly shut and breathing heavily; to allude that I was really asleep. Even at the age of two, instinctively I knew that something was not right. There was my daddy, alone with a woman who was not my mother; which made her a stranger to me. It is said that children can always sense the true nature of a person's spirit, and they will react accordingly when they do not trust the person's spirit. I mean, this situation was suspicious enough to make me want to pretend to be asleep, just so I could find out what was going on! What kind of child does this at the age of 2? This inquisitive nature would follow me into my later years. Into the room they came, and the first thing the lady says is, "Oh your baby is in here and she looks just like you!" My dad, who obviously did not wish to discuss the details of our family gene pool, callously responded "Yeah, but don't worry she sleep." The mystery woman then said, "What if she wakes up? Plus, she doesn't look sleep to me." My dad said, "She sleeps hard, watch." So he calls me by my name while shaking me. "Lil' girl … you woke?" That's what he called me sometimes. I start breathing even heavier now to convince my dad that I am knocked out. He says, "See… she is sound asleep". Then he picked me up and put me on the couch next to the bed.

Then he and the mystery lady proceeded to do what they came to do, while I pretended to be asleep on the couch.

I never told my dad how many times I replayed that moment in my mind or how it affected me as a child. I simply locked it away and put it in a place that I did not visit very often in my mind. I knew that my dad loved me and we had a very close relationship as I was growing up. He adored me and in my eyes, he could do no wrong. He was my dad, and I was his lil' girl.

I understand why it is so important for girls to have a healthy relationship with their fathers. Fathers are the first for a girl. He is her first love. Her father initially gauges a daughter's expectations of true love or extreme resentment for men. Dads, daddies and fathers (preferably) are the prototype and premise of all of her future relationship(s) with men, boyfriends and eventually, her husband. Her first perceptions about what constitutes a provider, a friend, a protector, or even an enemy, are from her father. My dad was truly my world. When I was full of innocence and did not know any better, I remained unaffected by the hurtful things he did to my mother. I felt he had not done anything wrong to me because he treated me the same, unconditionally as always.

My mom on the other hand, wasn't so crazy about him. She never really had anything good to say about him. I am sure it is because of the hurt and pain he caused her in their marriage. Whenever we would mention his name, she did not seem to like it very much.

In fact, the slightest mention of his name would send her over the edge. She would say things like "Y'all think your dad is so perfect don't you?" So to keep the peace we stopped talking about him around her. You see my mom and dad separated early in their marriage. My mother found out about dad and the mystery woman through me and after a while, she just could not take him or his philandering ways anymore. She clearly had reached the limit of her tolerance for his infidelity. So she packed us up and moved us out of state, far away from him. Sadly, that actually turned out to be the last time I saw my dad for a long period of time. When I told my mom about that lady in the bed with him and the noises they were making while I laid there on the couch, she cried justifiably. She told him that he would never see his kids again and believe me, she did everything in her power to make that possible. My dad wasn't giving up so easy though. He eventually found out where she had moved to and he came to Milwaukee, Wisconsin, which is where we relocated. He came bearing an abundance of gifts for us kids and he gave my mom money to take care of us. This was all done in an effort to win her over and get her back. However, his attempts were futile because it never happened. Once mom said she was done, she never looked back.

I often thought about my dad as a little girl. I had a friend who would come by and visit me all the time. Her name was Tracy. I idolized this girl. I thought that she had it made. She wore the best clothes and she had the latest and best of everything. She even had both parents at home. At that time, I actually began looking for someone to befriend me so I would not have to stay at home all of the time. Although it is considered a societal norm, one of the saddest things a child can ever experience is the emotional turmoil of being the product of a broken home. I was becoming a latchkey kid. Life at home was changing drastically. When mom left dad, she had lost a mate but she had gained a social life.

Home did not feel like home anymore. Mom fancied herself as the world's greatest hostess, and our house was one big party hall, Party Central! I believe she was feeling quite empty inside since the dissolution of her marriage, and filling her house with those people helped mask the emptiness that was growing within her. There were numerous people at my mom's house partying all night long until the wee hours of the morning. Sometimes, when my mother would finish putting us to bed, I would get picked up and moved from the bed where my two brothers slept to another room by one of the guests who regularly came by to party with her. He was a family member who was related to us through marriage not by blood. That particular room was always scary to me because no matter how loud I would cry, the music was much louder. My cries of terror were suffocated by the music so no one ever heard me, or came for me in there. It was in that room…things happened to me in there that caused me to put my mind, my emotions, my heart and soul in the same place where I hid my dad's basement affair… that dark, torrid, secret place that I never cared to revisit…ever.

Sometimes I wish these memories were not so vivid, because no one person should have to store and keep gross, unpleasant memories from such a tender and innocent age. I was three years old when it all started but I remember who the man was and exactly what he was doing to me. This was the first sexual experience that I can remember. I was the unwilling participant of non-consensual oral sex, performed on me by an adult male and I could do nothing about it. I was an unsuspecting, unprotected child, who had no idea of what or why this was happening to me. Could you imagine what I was going through? Well for your sake reader, I hope you cannot.

Because no child, no girl, no woman, no person should ever have to experience the trauma and anguish of this horrific violation.

You see, putting those memories away allowed me to be free and that is who I was. I was a free soul. I was happy and full of joy all the time, from the day I was born. I was just a happy carefree little girl. I hid those things in secret and never talked about it, mainly because I was confused. I was an innocent victim, never really sure if what happened to me was wrong. I mean, these were adults right? Adults knew what was right and what was wrong right? Grown people would never steer you wrong, right? Well I found out the hard way that they do, especially those who are confused themselves.

I just knew not to talk about it because I was told not to. I remember trying to walk to school with my oldest brother. Like older brothers, he was always trying to protect me. So one day I got up one morning while he was getting dressed to walk down the street for school. I dressed myself at the age of four and followed behind him the whole way, to the "big boy" school. He kept telling me that I was too young for school but I wasn't even trying to hear him, so I kept walking! Imagine the shock of the staff when they seen this non-registered, eager, headstrong little girl marching in their building, demanding them to let her do what the big kids do! Once we got to the school the teacher took me into the office where they called my mom. She had no idea that I was even gone from the house because she was still sleeping in from partying all night long. She came to pick me up and took me back home, but she never asked me why I did that. She simply told me, "Honey you'll get your chance to go to school real soon."

At this young age of four I was trying to escape the life of what was happening around me. My oldest brother was always someone I could trust and following him to school made me feel comfortable, as I was always thinking of ways to not be at home because of the evil that was occurring there. My mother telling me that I would get my chance only created a sense of lost hope because the chance to go to school felt like it would take years to come.

CHAPTER THREE – PICTURE PERFECT TURNAROUND

The year is 1979 I'm about seven years old, thin as a nail, with short, sandy red hair, and full of life. I am realizing how much I really love to sing! It seemed like everywhere I went I was trying to sing a song to whomever would listen. I thought I was the best singer on this side of heaven. When I was about four or five years old, my mother would take me to the bar with her sometimes and she would let me sing for the customers. Oh, those people went gaga over this little girl singing Natalie Cole's "Love on my Mind," with the emotional conviction of a seasoned singer! Sometimes the men would give me money that my mom would keep for me. I was enthralled that these people enjoyed receiving my gift as much as I enjoyed giving it!

Looking back I could see why some veteran and legendary singers find it hard to let go of the spotlight when they are past their prime. Sometimes we watch them on television or see them in concert, and we cringe at every note they sing. "He needs to hang it up". "She can't sing like she used to." "They know they're too old for that now!" But the attention is like a drug. It is only human nature for us to become absorbed in the adoration because when God gave us gifts, He gave them to us to share them with the world.

So when I was up there singing, I felt like I mattered, so I wanted to keep singing! The money only increases the singer's need to sing! I got used to the attention pretty quickly, and I decided that I wanted to be a singer when I grew up.

Teachers would always ask the students what they wanted to be when they grew up in class, and the students would answer with the textbook career responses: a doctor, a nurse, a police officer a fireman etc. Me, I would always say the same thing. "I want to be a singer!" I would constantly get the same response from the teachers, "That is not a realistic goal Olivia." Even though it seemed like people were always telling me what I was going to be and what I should not be, I continued to dream the same dream.

Pretty soon, schools were sending out sponsor letters to my mom to have me attend special schools for the gifted and talented to nurture my gift. But my mother was so afraid of letting me go.

To this day, I am not sure why she flat out refused to let me go. I certainly proved that I was more than qualified for the opportunity.

She had no problem with me showcasing my gift in all the WRONG places (bars & taverns), and for monetary gain at that! These schools were the perfect platform for me to learn and grow. These places could have built the foundation for my future I thought for sure she would have been overjoyed, ready and willing for me to partake in something so exciting and beneficial. If for nothing else, I would have been attending the school to sing! Singing was my dream, my passion, and my sanctuary! Maybe she felt there was some unknown threat or danger that I was overlooking.

Maybe she thought she was protecting me in that regard. I have spent countless days pondering over her questionable motives. Despite her efforts, it seemed as if I found more danger at home!

Soon I began missing one opportunity after another and eventually I became just like the other kids. When the teacher would ask, "What do you want to be when you grow up?"

I, now being systematically programmed on what to say and what not to say, gave the same textbook response, "I want to be a nurse." Sure enough, they were fully satisfied. I knew what I was doing. I was saying what they wanted to hear, but in my mind I would say, "One day I'm going to be a singer and I'm going to do it for God!" But until then I better try to please the people around me because that is what will make them like me. "I went along, to get along." I would eventually find out that this mentality would do more harm to me than good.

My mother was completely over my father and she was ready to test the waters of love again. Around this time, she had fallen in love with a man named "Spade". They were inseparable. She seemed happier than she had been in a long time. After a long courtship, things had gotten really serious between them and one day, Spade moved in with us. How great was that? It was just what I wanted. I finally had what I have been missing for so long. I felt like Tracy and I were on the same level now.

We were now looked at as a real family. We were the first family on the block to have cable (cable was a real true luxury back in day). We had a big, classic 25-inch floor model Curtis Mathes color television set and everyone used to come to our house to watch the fights and the big games. We had one of the most beautiful homes in the neighborhood and it was filled with love. Believe me, that was something big back then. It meant everything. It saddens me that God's model of the traditional family is on the endangered species list today.

You see having a mother and a father in a home together was the standard. The sentiment was even reflected on television. Families ate together at the kitchen table, and they did everything together. It just was the way things were back then, and it is God's original design for the family. It was to be expected, and it was the norm. I finally felt like our home was complete.

To reiterate, our house was now a home. Now in the beginning I had a hard time with Spade trying to step up and play daddy, so I was very mean spirited and defiant toward him and in a sense, I felt justified. In the back of my mind, I kept saying, "He ain't my daddy!" But that was only because I felt that he was trying to take my dad's place, and my heart always belonged to my dad. I would do things to Spade to get him angry hoping that it would make him leave. I basically played him and my mom against each other for the first couple of years of their relationship, simply because I could. Spade had to let me get away with it because he had to get us to accept him so he could stay with mom. He needed our approval. I made several attempts to split them up, but I failed miserably! I finally gave up when I realized and accepted that my efforts were not going to work.

Once I realized that Spade wasn't going anywhere and he genuinely loved my mom and her kids, I began to let up on him a bit. Every now and then I'd still throw the "You're not my daddy!" out there but over all, I really enjoyed the family time with him.

You see, Spade had a large family; he had four brothers and five sisters and most of them had kids that my brothers and I played with. There was always somewhere to go and something to do. We even went to family reunions every year as if we were actually a part of their family. Once we went down to Jackson, Tennessee to visit some of Spade's family members, who happened to own a farm. I had never been on a farm before and for some reason, I thought I would really like it. I would always tell my mom that I wanted a pet cow until I actually saw one in real life. I remember walking over to the cow. I tried several times to pet her, but I could never get my hand to make contact.

The moment finally came to make my attempt. I stuck my eager hand out to touch her thick, smooth skin, and moo she went... and running I went! I guess at that point she sounded as if she said move and that is exactly what I did! When nighttime came, I was terrified. The nights were so dark, scary, and pitch black. You couldn't even see your hand if it was right in front of your face. There was not a streetlight or anything for miles, just total darkness. I didn't like darkness for many reasons. I remember the morning Spade's uncle, who we called Uncle Don, went outside and killed a pig that we were playing with the day before, and cooked it! Everybody ate it, except me. I couldn't. I was too sad for the pig. I have always been very sensitive, and eating that pig would have felt as if I was attending a friend's execution. With the big bugs, "moving" cows, strange sounds in the night, the assassination of pets, and all of the darkness, I realized that I really hated being there and I could not wait to get back to the city! I am a CITY GIRL and proud of it!

In the summertime we would have barbeques at home, and the whole family would attend. We would even have kid parties with all the kids from Spade's family and ours. The adults played cards, drank and listened to music.

In my home we had family night once a week, where my mom and Spade would let my two brothers and I entertain them for an hour or so. Those were some good times. My eldest brother, who had the rhythm of a coat rack, would dance to my mother's delight. His signature move was Michael Jackson's moonwalk. My mother would just love it, while my little brother and I would crack up with laughter. My little brother would tell corny jokes that were not funny in the comedic sense, but they were amusing because they made no sense at all. The whole family would laugh so hard until tears were streaming down our faces. And me? Of course I would sing. I would stand in the middle of the floor as if it was my stage, and sing my little heart out.

After my dad left, Spade was the only father figure that my brothers and I had ever known. My older brother, for some reason, was really attached to Spade. He made up in his mind that Spade was his real father. For Spade to not be our biological father, he and my brother shared similar facial features. Knowing this was like an added bonus for us. It sweetened the pot. It legitimized us as a real family unit. I was convinced and reassured at that moment, that family means everything.

Finally, I thought, I had a real complete family, with a grandmother and all. My grandparents on both parents' sides died when I was just a toddler so I never knew what it felt like to have grandparents. Spade's mom was the very best! She had to be the kindest woman I have ever known.

Everybody called her 'mama' or 'Ms. Love' and to this day I understand why. This lady was the epitome of love. She made my brothers and I feel as if we were her very own grandchildren from the day she met us.

It was always so many of us together that no one was ever bold or foolish enough to pick a fight or mess with us. We were thick as thieves and if anyone would ever catch one of us alone, the outcome would always be the same. It could be seconds later, and the word was out! Like a swarm of bees, a squad of us would be on the scene; and it would be ugly for those unfortunate souls from that point on! It sure feels good to belong, to be a part of something. The security of knowing that you are protected, knowing that you matter and knowing that people care about you is truly incomparable. There was never a dull moment in those days. My life was full and complete, growing up with family. Frankly, security had been a deficient element in our family and it would have been totally depleted if Spade had not come into my mom's life. He definitely filled the void. He was pretty laid back for the most part. He sure liked his drink though. He always kept something in his back pocket. He never tried to really discipline me but he would whip my brothers every now and then.

I do remember an incident that occurred one day when my brothers and I were watching television. Spade and my mom came home and right in the middle of our program Spade, (being the man of the house) walked over to the TV and changed the channel. His favorite TV show was Hogan's Heroes. I absolutely hated this program! I hated the theme music so much that every time it would come on, I would get upset just by the sound of the music alone. Not to mention the characters and their bad acting. The show was just starting and Spade wanted to watch it.

Well on this day I was not in the mood, and I was not having it. I was a sassy ten year old with the heart of a soldier. I was never quick to back down from anything or anyone. I was the leader of the pack with in my "clique" of friends, and I carried that title at home as well! So when he turned the channel, I got right up, went over to the TV and turned the channel back to the show that we were watching (this battle would have been easier with a remote control, but we did not have one back then). Boy did that make him upset. He said to me, "If you touch that TV again I'm gone whoop you." So he walked back to the TV and turned the channel. Now mind you, he never whipped me, plus my mom was in the room too; so I knew she was not going to let him lay a finger on me. So I walked right back over to the TV and turned the channel back again. I could tell this was not going to go my way, but it wasn't going to go his way either. Not today!

Suddenly, he snatched off his leather belt and threatened to whip me with it. Being a fierce and defiant ten year old, I challenged him by ripping the phone cord right from the wall and indicating, "If you hit me I'm going to hit you back." He was so angry "Oh yeah" he said, then POP... he hit me. True to my word, with all of my might I hit him with the phone cord right across his back (by the way he wasn't wearing a shirt at the time either, OUCH!) So hit me again, and I hit him again. This tug of war went on for a few minutes until he said to my mom, "You better get your daughter!" I said, "Mama you better get your man!" My mom, who was just sitting there watching, took a minute to gather her thoughts. She said, "Okay that's enough!" in a loud voice. Spade and I stood toe to toe starring each other down. Then he walked away.

That night no one watched anything and both shows were over. It took a couple days to pass before we made up but we did, and I apologized. By this time I had mastered the game of people pleasing. I would tell people what they wanted to hear, I did what they wanted me to do, and I kept their dirty little secrets.

Realizing that grown-ups sometimes had some pretty messed up ways, I thought if I would act more grown up, I would get more privileges and more respect from them. So I would sit at the bottom of the stairs to listen to how they would talk to one another, or I would sit quietly in my room hoping to listen in on their conversations. I would mimic them, repeat the words that they said, and acted as if I knew exactly what they were talking about. Boy was I ever wrong! It only made matters worse. I was constantly in adults' faces trying to behave like them or trying to talk like them, and it would make my mom furious. She would say things like, "Get out of my face and stop acting so grown!" Or in other words, stop trying to act grown because you are not, and stay in a child's place.

CHAPTER FOUR – LUCKY 11

It is July 29th, 1983. It is my 11th birthday. This birthday brings back many memories. For starters, Mother Nature caught me off guard, which made me very uncomfortable with myself because my mother never gave me the mother daughter talk about "the road to puberty." I started menstruating on my eleventh birthday. I remember that awful call I had to make to my mom on the phone to tell her that I was bleeding from "down there". My mom was silent for a moment then said, "Well, this is what you do." She told me to go into the hallway cabinet, get a maxi pad out the box, go into the bathroom, peel the sticky part off and put it on, so I did. When she came home she asked me to come into the bathroom to see if I needed to change it, only to find that I had attached the sticky part to me! I wasn't sure of how to use it. But in my mind, it was a big band-aid. So of course, I put the sticky part on me to stop the bleeding. My mother laughed and said, "No honey, let me get another one and I will show you how to use it." She looked into the box to find it empty. "What did you do? Where are all my pads?" "I used them." I said. Again, in my mind, I thought they were band-aids so I had to keep changing them because, well you know, to stop the bleeding. I knew nothing about what was happening to me. I never had the talk with my mother, nor did anyone else tell me about the changes a young girl's body goes through. My mother just looked at me, shaking her head. She went into her room to get some more maxi pads then showed me how to use them.

Years earlier before my mother met Spade, she went out with a man named Randy, who stayed in touch with her even though they were not dating anymore. He was always very nice to us, so my mom trusted him around us and occasionally she would even let us go by and visit him.

Even though I made it painfully clear to any man who dated my mom that he was not my dad, Randy would always agree and would reassure us that he was not trying to be.

Randy had told me to make sure I come by on my birthday to pick up my birthday gift from him. So, later that day a couple of my friends and I walked to his house to get my birthday present from him. To my surprise we got there only to find that he did not have it. I was so disappointed.

But to make it up to me, he said he was going to take my friends and me to Burger King for ice cream, and he was going to give me $11 (one dollar for every year of my age). So we piled in his car to go get ice cream. Randy drove us to Burger King, which was right up the street from his house, and we went in. He ordered 3 big cones but only paid for two. He said he must have left his other wallet with my birthday money in it at home, and he did not have enough money to pay for all three cones so we would have to go back to the house to get it. So he told my friends to stay and eat their ice cream and we would be right back. Where were my "adult" instincts then? They should have been kicking in because something surely was not "kosher" with this situation. But again, I was still a child, trying to be grown and my naïveté was in full control. Looking back, I know now that there was no way in the world that we were supposed to be meeting with that man alone, and without a trusted adult present.

Excited about my birthday money, I jumped in the front seat of the car. I began to roll the window down because this was a very hot day in July. As he began driving, he said to me, "You know I love you don't you?" "Yes", I replied. "And you know I would never hurt you right"? Again I replied. "Yes," but this time I felt a strange feeling in my stomach. It was a nervous, queasy feeling. It was as if someone was twisting it in small knots. Slowly driving through an alley he said to me, "I'm going to make a quick stop and then we'll go and get your birthday money okay"? "Okay", I replied in a sad voice thinking to myself, God please don't let him hurt me.

He pulled into a garage just up the street from his house, and asked me to take off my shorts. I passionately responded, "No! My mama told me never to take off my clothes for anyone!" He said, "I'm not going to hurt you I just want to rub up against you." He then pulled his penis out of his pants and started groping himself. I said, "I'm bleeding down there." He was shocked and grossly excited to hear this, and with piqued curiosity, he said, "Let me see!" I couldn't believe that he was this kind of man! I felt angry, violated, disgusted and terrified all at the same time. Fearfully, I said "No!" again and began to cry. "Okay, okay" he said. "Just get on your knees then." "No!" I said. With tears streaming down my face I said to God, "Please help me." At that point, I believe God came and took that episode of my life and threw it into the sea of forgetfulness, His and mine.

I never had a complete memory of what actually happened that day, and I thank God for that. All I know is, when I came back from wherever I had drifted off to, he was standing outside the car in the garage "draining himself" (ejaculating). I remember pulling up my shorts and sitting there quietly. Then just as he had promised, he stopped by his house, got the eleven dollars and took me to Burger King's drive thru as if nothing ever happened! I remember on the way home he said to me "If you tell anyone what happened, I'm going to kill you and your family, do you understand?"

Looking into his eyes, I felt empty inside. I responded, "Yes, I understand."

The next few days I was very withdrawn. I am not sure if it was because I could not remember what had happened or if it was the threat that he put on my family, but either way I was not myself, and I knew it. My oldest brother kept saying to me, "What's wrong with you?" I would say, "Nothing." He would say, "Something's wrong and I'm gone call mama and tell her if you don't tell me." I kept saying, "Nothing's wrong with me, leave me alone!" My brother did exactly what he said he was going to do he called my mom.

At the time my mom was over her sister's house. My brother said "Mama something is wrong with Livy she's crying and she won't talk, she just keeps saying there's nothing wrong, but it is." My mom asked my brother to put me on the phone but as soon as I heard her voice all I could do was cry profusely. My mom got upset because I would not talk but the truth was that I could not talk. I could not utter a single word. So she came home and looked at me in my face with a look of great concern. She said, "Tell me what's wrong! Did something happen to you?" So I mustered up the words, "Randy raped me on my birthday." After those words left my mouth, it seemed like the whole world stood still. Saying it out loud was as if I was finally admitting it to myself that it actually happened. My mother started shaking her head violently and began saying "No, no, no!" then she began to cry. She grabbed me and held me really tight and said, "Don't you worry about a thing, everything is going to be all right!" First, she called the police then she called Randy. He did not kill me, or my family for that matter, but something inside me knew that he really wanted to. The doctors said there was no penetration, which made my mom relax a bit knowing that at eleven years old her daughter was still a virgin and there was no chance of me being pregnant. So maybe he really did all that he said that he wanted to do (rub up against me). The police collected the evidence they needed from the garage so they were able to arrest him.

My mom sent me to Michigan to stay with my aunt for a while. She would periodically visit me while I was there and she would always take me to see my dad. I remember staying in the hotel with him the evening that I arrived in Michigan. We stayed up talking about random subjects, just shooting the breeze when suddenly, my mind drifted back into the garage; that awful scene of the crime where all things became blank.

My dad asked, "you all right lil' girl?" I looked at him and said, "Randy raped me!" I remember my dad became speechless for a moment then, he said, "He raped you?" I responded, "Yeah. In a garage on my birthday, and I was on my period daddy." Then out of nowhere my daddy began to cry, so I started crying too. My dad picked me up and held me really tight and said, "You'll never have to worry about him again. I promise." That familiar sense of protection and security was temporarily present within me again because my father assured me that it would never happen again. Little did daddy know that I would need more than his words to block the dangers that were lurking in the distance, I needed supernatural protection from the demons that were waiting to slay me.

I often wondered what was it about me that made people do these unspeakable things. I never knew or understood why. I could never seem to grasp why the evil spirit of perversion hovered, haunted and preyed upon me. It was nothing that I asked for, and I did not do anything to welcome it. Yet I seemed to attract every perverted devil on the earth. It was as if "that family member" was the king predator and marked his territory on me and sent smoke signals and pheromones to the vultures of prey to devour whatever was left of me. Just a few months after that incident one of my mom's close friends became a boogie-woman in the middle of the night.

It took her a long time to get my mom to agree to let me spend the night with her and her children because she had all boys. My mom would always say, "What is she going to do over there? Plus she won't have anyone to play with." Well, the woman told my mom that she wanted to take me shopping for a bathing suit and let me swim in her pool. She had the biggest pool I had ever seen in back of her house. She was always buying gifts for us kids and giving us money. I guess you could say she was a wealthy woman. After many attempts and requests, she was finally able to convince my mom to give in, and she allowed me to spend the night. She had taken me shopping for a bikini just as she had promised. She let me model by the pool just like the professional models. She told me that I was the prettiest little girl and some day I would grow up to be an even prettier lady. I really thought she was the best. All of the kids called her Auntie June because that is what she wanted us to call her. I was never big on swimming but I loved receiving gifts! So I pretended to swim in the pool along with her three sons, who were very close to me in age. The night was winding down so she said I could sleep in her bed with her.

That night I woke up to find her kissing and licking me between my legs while looking into the video camera, which she was using earlier that day to film us while we were swimming. She had taken off my bathing suit so I was completely naked. I remember while putting on the suit, she was taking pictures of me while the video camera was recording. I was so happy about my new bathing suit that I did not think anything of it. Her breasts were exposed while I was putting on the suit, and she was very comfortable in her nakedness, unlike my mom; who would always say, "Turn around!" when she would undress in front of me. I remember June saying to me, "this is what girls do when they are alone together."

She proceeded to lie on top of me and began grinding on me as if she was a man. She then began to moan out loud. Then she said we had to keep that night a secret. "You can't even tell your mom." I would often wonder if these people loved me, why they would say that they never wanted to hurt me, yet always wanted me to keep these things a secret.

Why couldn't I share these encounters with my family and my parents of all people? Why were these requests always supplemented by gifts, bribes and "hush money?" Why did I always feel so bad throughout the duration of these experiences? Why do I black out if everything is indeed appropriate behavior?

Anyway, Auntie June said, "We're going shopping in the morning to buy you something pretty okay?" Okay I replied as I lied in the bed looking at her. That memory of us stayed right there in that room, for 25 years. God hid that memory from me for years so my mother never even knew what happened to me that evening; not even to this day. Maybe she will find out once she reads this book. Strangely enough, June was involved in a horrible car accident and died. Sometimes I wonder if that was God's way of punishing her. There is no telling if she molested other girls before me, but I will never know. She was a very friendly woman, but she was operating in the wrong spirit behind closed doors. Somehow I managed to suppress that memory for years.

One evening my family was watching a movie on our coveted cable television. We did that once a week as a family. When the movie went off I said to my mom, "I'm going to be just like her". I remember my mom asking me what I meant by that. So I replied, "I was going to be a call girl at $500.00 a whop. Then I'm going to be a gospel singer like Mahalia Jackson." I remember my mom's mouth dropped and she said "Don't you ever say that again you hear me?" "Yes ma'am," I said confused. I wasn't sure why she was so mad.

Olivia Jackson

In my mind and in my recent experiences, people like to give you things in exchange for sex. So I figured I was not going to have sex unless I was getting paid like the woman in the movie. I could tell that my resolution did not go over as well as I thought it would. The look on my mother's face was one of sheer disappointment. So I said, "Mama I was just kidding" in hopes to make her happy. But something inside of me was still very much intrigued by the movie.

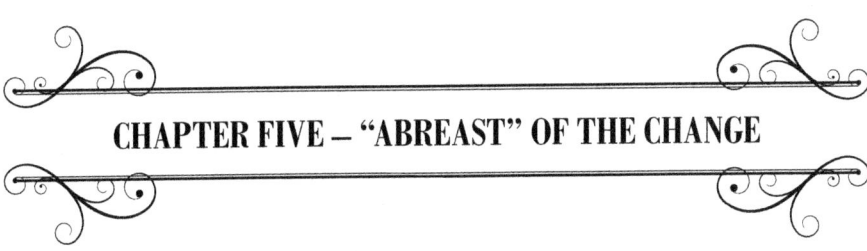

CHAPTER FIVE – "ABREAST" OF THE CHANGE

I am thirteen now. I finally made it to the teenage years! I should have been greeted with a sign that read, "Welcome to a Whole New Set of Problems!" At this time and age, things began to change in our home. Things also began to change in the neighborhood. I was fighting more and more. I was getting jumped by groups of girls who thought that I was acting as if I was better than they were, simply because of the way I looked. I was always a pretty girl, and a girly and prissy girl at that. But now I had something that most girls my age just did not have. I remember waking up one morning with a full set of boobs! I freaked! I screamed, "MOM COME IN HERE!" I was so afraid to come out of my bedroom because I did not want my brothers to see me. My mom said, "You come here, what's wrong with your legs?" "No!" I shouted! "You come here!"

Reluctantly, my mom walked into my bedroom. "This better be good...what is it Livy?" she said annoyingly. I said, "Look!" "Look at what?" I moved my covers down and out popped this full set of breasts. With a surprised face she said, "I'm going to have to get you a training...I'm going to have to get you a bra!" I literally went from a flat chest to a 36C overnight, and from that moment on I literally lost connection with myself.

In school I became very popular, all the guys wanted to know if my boobs were real. They went as far as to pay some of the girls to find out. I was so embarrassed by them that I hid myself. During gym class I would always pretend to be on my menstrual just so I did not have to shower with the rest of the girls. My breasts were larger than some of the instructors!

Talk about going through the dreaded awkward stages! Some girls cannot wait to grow breasts when they are teens. I was just the opposite, I already had enough going on and it only made me miserable. My breasts would always say, "look at me" even when I did not want to be seen. They also betrayed my true age and made me look older than I actually was. That created even more drama for me. Once the boys found out that they were real, I had guys lining up hoping to become my boyfriend. But once the girls found out they were real they became insecure around me and jealous because all the attention I would get from the boys/men.

By now my oldest brother became very over-protective of me. He was always fighting or getting into it with someone over me. He hated for me to even walk near him and his friends because he knew they would be staring at my boobs. Every time I walked outside I would get all of this unwanted attention from the men in the neighborhood. My mom was constantly saying, "She's only thirteen!" in a voice that said back off! It would temporarily take the attention off of me.

You would think that all this unwanted attention was enough, but nope there's more. The devil never misses an opportunity to stir up trouble. The tides started shifting between my parents at this time too.

It seemed like my mom and dad were fighting more often. My mom was working two jobs at this point and between working and partying all the time, she seemed to not have any time for the family, so I became the mom.

I did the cooking, cleaning, and the laundry for my brothers and me. And without warning, the trends of the eighties found their way into our home. Hard drugs crept into our house or should I say into my mom's life. Since we were not aware of the signs, traits and innuendos of drug addicts, we were very naïve to the behavior and influence that we would eventually see in her. Almost instantly drugs began affecting our entire family and it extended past the walls of our home. Publicly, we were on display, we went from being the family who had it all on the block, to the family who had nothing at all, over night. We were falling apart at the seams and our personal lives were in shambles.

I was still singing to who ever wanted to hear me. And just when I thought no one would ever notice me or recognize my talent; my music teacher asked if I would sing Whitney Houston's huge hit, "The Greatest Love of All" at my eighth grade graduation ceremony. I did not think I could pull it off, so I asked my aunt to help me practice. I worked overtime practicing with my aunt Gladys. She was tough and she would not let up on me because she knew that I could do it. She had faith in me when I did not have it in myself.

Finally the day arrived and to my surprise I knocked that song out the box! I didn't know how gifted I was and my mom didn't know either. As a matter of fact I didn't even know until that day! I have never heard myself through a microphone before. There wasn't a dry eye in the auditorium. Everyone was crying and was visibly moved by the song, and the passion behind it. "LEARNING TO LOVE YOURSELF IT IS THE GREATEST LOVE OF ALL!" I will never forget that day, it was one of the greatest memories of my youth. I realized that I had an amazing gift and I wanted to share it with the world. But somehow my mom did not want to share that dream with me. She was always trying to keep me close to her instead of nurturing my God given gift.

Everyone would ask, "What high school are you going to in the fall?" "Marshall" I said. They would respond, "Why? You should go to West Division; it's the school for the arts." Well, I never knew that because no one really showed any interest in my gift until that day. The school I attended took no interest in my gift and unfortunately it was too late, in order to go to the school of the arts you had to start there in your freshmen year. Since I never followed a trained path, "Train up a child in the way they should go and when they get old they will not depart from it" - Proverbs 22:6. Since I never followed a trained path, I became a follower of my peers, regrettably. My gift was miscarried (it died, prematurely) because of a lack of knowledge. "My people perish from a lack of knowledge."- Hosea 4: 6

Coming home from high school one day, I walked in to see Spade packing his things and moving out. I didn't know what happened that made him leave or if my mom had put him out, but it was apparent that the love affair was over. He left and never came back, without any explanation. Not again I thought. It really bothered me, just when I was getting use to being a complete family with full acceptance this happens. It seemed to hurt my eldest brother the most because he had a bond with Spade that my younger brother and I did not share with him. Spade would take my older brother just about everywhere with him and that made their relationship so much stronger. I think it was probably because we knew our biological dad but my eldest brother didn't know his.

He had received a picture of him when he was a young kid but he had never seen him in person.

My eldest brother had to become the man of the house. He was now responsible for protecting the family, but mostly me because I was the only girl. I think my brother resented my "metamorphosis" more than me! He was very mean to me, and he made me feel that it was my fault that I developed so early. Even though I did not show it like he did, I was greatly distressed over the separation of our family.

Shortly after Spade left, my big brother started to drink all of the time. He would even drink during school hours, sometimes to the point of passing out. I remember once he even drank until he poisoned himself by mixing different alcohol beverages, and ended up in the hospital. I am not sure if it was because he was hurting over of the breakup of our family, or if he just picked up a bad habit following the footsteps of his friends. It seemed like we were both following the wrong crowd.

Not long after that I was in my mothers' room cleaning up. I was hoping to earn some money so I could go to the store with my friends. I found a tray under her bed with pipes and other things on it that I was unfamiliar with, so I showed it to my big brother. He said he did not know what it was, but he just knew that it was not good. But I could tell he could not wait to confront my mom about it. She denied that it was even hers, but my brother refused to let up. So he got angry and even called her out of her name. He said that he was leaving and he was never coming back. At the age of sixteen, my oldest brother walked away from our family, never to return again, leaving my youngest brother and myself to fend for ourselves. I could not believe it. It seemed like the men in my family had an expiration date on them. My mother was using street drugs and they were starting to rule and ruin her life.

Suddenly, nothing meant more to her than getting high. It had gotten so bad that she began to sell all of our furniture out of the house just to get high. Shortly after, my mom went on welfare and my little brother and I started stealing food and clothes in order to keep going. With Spade and my eldest brother gone, it was just us three. When my mother was in her zone, it felt like just us two – my brother and me. My life had completely flipped upside down within a matter of weeks. I became very angry and confused. I was not sure where my life was headed. My relationship with my mom was changing... for the worse. We used to be the best of friends. Now we were barely speaking to each other. There was no more quality time, no family fun nights, and no sober mom to have any kind of mother daughter talks. I felt alone and vulnerable with no one to turn to. Where could I go? I thought about the time when I thought that those feminine napkins were band aids, used to stop the bleeding, now I needed a band aid to cover my heart. Who or what could stop this bleeding?

CHAPTER SIX – THE IMMACULATE DECEPTION

It is now the winter of 1986. I am on the bus stop with my friend Dee waiting on the city bus to go to school. It was freezing outside. A neighbor from across the street pulled up to the corner lowered his window and asked, "Y'all need a ride?" I looked at Dee and said, "My mom told him to stay away from me. She told me she did not like the way he looks at me." "No, that's okay!" I shouted. Dee said "Girl its cold out here! He won't try anything with both of us in the car, come on!" The "friendly" neighbor said "Come on I'll give y'all a ride to school." Against my better judgment I got in the car and before Dee could get one leg in, he pulled off from the curb! The door of the car was still swinging open. Shocked and enraged I said, "Why would you do that?" He said, "Because I want to show you something plus I don't know her." He said, "Don't worry I'm still taking you to school." "I can't be late." I said. "Okay it won't take long". So he continued driving until he pulled up to this house. He then got out of the car and said, "Come on in." I said "No! I got to get to school and I'm going to be late."

He opened the passenger door where I was and grabbed my arm lightly to reassure me that he did not have anything up his sleeve. "Come on its okay. You won't be late. "I got out the car and walked up the stairs. "I said I can't be late for school or I'll get in trouble", hoping to play on his conscience a bit. Suddenly he stopped responding. He just looked at me. I knew I was in trouble because I had a tight knot in the pit of my stomach.

It was the same knotting and gnawing pain that I felt when Randy violated me. My heart felt like it was crying and I could do nothing about it. This memory is so clear that I still remember the clothing I had on. I was wearing a blue jean skirt with leg warmers and a little bomber jacket, the typical eighties teenage girl gear. I will never forget what I wore that day because I changed clothes down the street at a friend's house after leaving home. Like most girls at that age, I borrowed clothes from my girlfriends because my clothes were not the trendiest due to everything that was going on in my home.

My mom was spending all of her money on drugs, and not on clothes for my brother and me. We were on welfare and I didn't get to shop anymore, so most of my clothes looked and were recycled.

So in order for me to continue going to school half way decent I would either wear my friends' clothes or steal them.

Anyhow, when I got to the top of the stairs he said, "Wait right here, I'll be back." For a minute, I actually thought he really had something to show me. You would think by now, I would know better but I didn't. It was deja vu of Burger King all over again. My young mind wasn't mature enough to recognize the signs. I realized that he was getting a key from someone else in the building. This was a room and board house so when he came back he said, "Come on." I hesitated, and then I began to feel more afraid because I didn't know what to do. He said, "Quit acting shy girl, come on." I believe my legs froze in place because he literally pulled me in the room while I was pleading with him saying I have to go to school.

The first thing he asked me once I was in the room was; "Are you a virgin?" Since I was not sure what that even meant, I said, "I don't know." He said, "You don't know if you are one or you don't know what it means? "Both" I responded. He said, "Have you ever had sex?" I said, "No!" He smirked and said, "It won't hurt I promise." He sat down on the bed and said, "Here give me a hug." I stood there saying, "I have to go to school." I was so nervous I began to cry. He stood up and pushed me to the bed, and forcefully he began to rape me. There was blood on the bedspread and in between my legs. When he got off of me, surprisingly he said, "You were a virgin huh? "Its okay, don't cry. I'm going to take care of you, I promise" he said. "Here is my phone number, call me if you ever need anything okay? Fix your clothes I'm going to take you to school." He was just as cool and calm, as if he did not just commit one of the most horrific crimes in the world! There is no way I could find comfort from the words of a monster!

He stole my virtue. He took something that belonged to God. He took something that was reserved for my husband. He ignored my plea, my request, and my refusal. I felt as though I had no reason to live.

I often thought why me? What did I do to deserve this? How many other girls had he raped in that house? As loud as I screamed, no one came for me even though I heard voices and I knew someone else was there. I have heard that sexual predators can sense their victims and that's why some victims are abused repeatedly by multiple handlers. A deeper explanation explains that both abuser and victims are under the influence of deviant spirits-which is why they always cross paths.

I do not remember much about the ride to school, only the arrival. I asked him not to take me to the front door because I feared the kids would see me with him and talk about me riding with this grown man." So I asked him to take me to the side of the building to drop me off. I went into class and sat down. I didn't realize that blood had run down my legs and had dried up until my teacher called me in the hall and asked me if everything was okay.

I said, "I was raped by my neighbor." I spoke devoid of all emotions. A soulless, blank stare replaced the glow that was once always present in my eyes. I think I was more afraid of what my mom was going to do to me than anything else. I know some of the kids were listening at the door so they may have heard what I had said to the teacher because she yelled, "Get back in the classroom." She called down to the office and spoke with one of the aids. Shortly after Ms. White came and walked me down from class to the nurses' station where I waited for the police to come. They made a call to my mom and put me on the line with her. Just as I thought, she was very upset with me. I knew she was hurt but I felt like it was entirely my fault because I knew better than to get in the car with him, yet I did it anyway.

I told the police that he had given me his phone number, so they had me call him under false pretenses. They told me to tell him to come and pick me up because I did not want to stay at school. But the plan was to set him up for an arrest. He agreed to come pick me up from side entrance of the school, the same place where he dropped me off. He was quickly arrested and soon thereafter; prosecuted. And that was just the beginning of my living nightmare. After taking my statement the police drove my mom and I to the hospital.

The police ordered a rape kit procedure. As I sat there staring at the floor, the nurse walked back into the room and told my mom to have a seat. My mom said, "Why, what is it?" The nurse told my mom that they ran a pregnancy test and wanted me to come back for the results. I said, "I'm not pregnant! I'm not pregnant! Mama I'm not pregnant! Please believe me I never had sex before!" My mother was so hurt; I could see it in her eyes. She knew that I had no idea that they were talking about the rape. My young mind actually thought that the act of rape and actual sexual intercourse were two different things. For any young reader who does not understand the difference between the two, the physical act of sex and rape are one and the same. The only difference is that rape is the act of forced sexual intercourse without consent or permission. She asked the nurse was this the first time that I had sex, only to find out that it was, and I could potentially be pregnant. That is when I found out it only takes one time to have sex to get pregnant.

The next couple of weeks were the longest weeks of my life. I was waiting for the test results and praying to God that they would not be positive. The whole time I stayed home from school hoping that this would all die down by the time I returned. I tried to be optimistic about the results but my optimism was all in vain. The test results were positive. I remember we were sitting there, both my mom and I, devastated and crying. My mom had been very distant toward me in those last few weeks. She was not really talking to me. She just drank and got high. It was all she could do avoid the pain and despair of this trauma.

I remember one day she got up hugged me and said, "It's going to be alright. We'll get through this together." I could not believe that I was going to have a baby when I was just a baby myself. I prayed over and over, begging and pleading to God to not let this happen to me. Everyone was going to talk about me and think that I was "that kind of girl" when I really was not. My mom told everybody that I was pregnant! It was so embarrassing. I was so ashamed and I started skipping school. The doctor's office called to set another appointment for me to find out the due date and to schedule an ultrasound.

My mother and her friend were already making plans for the baby but I could never accept it. This could not be my fate. It was almost three months later and we were back in the doctors' office. As I was getting undressed, I repeatedly told my mom that there is no baby inside of me and I did not have any symptoms of pregnancy. She said, "You will soon." I lied on the table and waited for the doctor to come in. I tensed up when he and the nurse entered the room with this big machine that was used to see the baby. The doctor walked in and attempted to relax me because he could see the fear on my face. He explained what he was going to do and that it would be painless. As he looked into the monitor, his brows were furrowed with confusion. To everyone's shock he announced that there was no baby in my womb! My head lifted slowly, and my brows lifted in ultimate surprise.

"I'm not pregnant?' I repeated, incredulously. "It certainly appears that way" said the doctor. "I don't understand!" he said. "We took two tests but I see no baby here on the ultrasound monitor!" "Good news missy...you are not pregnant!" "Thank God!" I shouted. My mother seemed strangely disappointed but she smiled anyway. God heard my prayers and He saw fit to keep that baby in heaven.

The Bible speaks of the steps of a good man (woman) being ordered by God. I often believed that in spite of all the things that happened to me, I was a good person and God was with me - at least that is what I believed. I often prayed and asked God to watch over my family and me and keep us safe. Even though many may not understand the logic of this situation, but in many ways God did just that. Even with all I had gone through in my youth I still believed that one day, God would come for me and rescue me from all of the pain and misery.

CHAPTER SEVEN – TURNED OUT

Drugs had completely taken over my mother's life. We were living in an empty house. Beds were just about all we had left. With no real, functional mother figure and no father in the home, I turned to the streets and tried desperately to fill that void. I began to seek love and acceptance anywhere except for where it could actually be found. I thought if I could find someone to love me, take care of me, and buy me the things I wanted and needed; I would be much happier. Somehow I thought I would be able to take care of myself without my mom or dad, but was I ever wrong!

On this quest for love and acceptance, I found everything but. One blatant truth that I did find out the hard way was that as a teenager, I did not have a clue of how to take care of myself; and that all adults (even those in my own family) did not always have my best interests at heart.

The women I met would all tell me that my mom was no good and worthless. They would say I could call them mom, or big sister depending on how old they were. But no matter how hard they would try to slander my mother's character, something inside me could never forget the way we were. No one could make me stop loving her. I loved my mom for real so I made excuses for her addiction by saying that she had a nervous breakdown. That was my way of staying connected to my mom, plus I felt that it was an advantage for me and people would feel sorry for me and want to be a mother or big sister figure in my life.

I was just fourteen years old, but after the rape I knew that my life would never be the same, so I began following the older crowd. I started going to skip-out parties, smoking cigarettes and weed and I started drinking until I would pass out. It seemed as if addiction had wrapped its cold, steel chains around my family. I remember the day I met Donna. She was eleven years older than I was, a real pretty lady who took me under her wing. She would always tell me how pretty I was and how much I reminded her of herself when she was my age. She began calling me her little sister. Donna would allow me to do anything I wanted to do when I came over to her house. A lot of the kids skipped school to hang out over there, which is how I met her. Immediately she began to dress me and make me feel loved. I was very comfortable around her. Then she tried to hook me up with her younger brother. He was 19 and a freshman in college. He played basketball too, so to most girls he was a real catch. To top it all off she offered to let me stay at her house if I ever needed to get away. So of course I thought I had it made.

One morning I went over to Donnas' house instead of school, which is what I did on a regular basis. But this day she took me with her to someone else's house. When we got there, I felt a strange vibe in the room, and it wasn't because of the marijuana smoke. There were two men there who had very thick Jamaican accents. From the looks of things there was a lot going on in that room, to say the least. There was a table full of weed and other stuff that I was not too familiar with at all, and they were not trying to hide it. They had all kinds of different liquor to choose from and they told me to help myself to anything I wanted. It was as if no one ever noticed that I was fourteen or they simply did not care. Either way they welcomed me in as if I was on the same level as they were. I loved it! They recognized me as their equal. I was finally around some really cool people who would let me in. I felt welcomed, I felt respected and I felt important. I have not felt this good in a long time, so on that day, at that moment, I was going to indulge and give in to whatever they offered me.

The little girl with the attitude was finally accepted. I felt like an adult because they allowed me to do whatever they did with no complaints. These grown people were letting me be grown! So

I grabbed the biggest cup I could find and began to pour some of everything in it. I did not know at the time that this "concoction" is what they call a Boilermaker, and that I was about to get wasted!

As the music played we dance and we drank, we drank and we danced. Then suddenly the room began to spin in circles. I could not stop the spinning and I could tell that I was going to be sick. I called to Donna, "Help me, I'm sick!" Donna and one of the other men were in another room at the time, but when she heard me call out to her, she came in the room where I was and said, "Here let me help you." She helped me to my feet and held me up while walking me into the bathroom where she and the other guy were. Then she said, "Pull on this and it will stop you from getting sick, but don't swallow the smoke because it could make you feel worse."

As I reflect on this life altering moment, the strange thing about it all is that even though Donna was doing more harm than good to me, she still somehow wanted to help me by giving me instructions to keep me from feeling worse. I had no idea what it was that she was giving me but I knew I did not like the way I was feeling at that moment and would have done anything to make that feeling go away. So I took a puff on the glass pipe that she was holding in front of me. To this day I cannot describe how I felt. I can only say that I drifted away from reality for a moment and when I came back, I could not speak. I never said another word. I just sat on the bathroom floor waiting on her to give me more. I had no clue that

I had just been introduced to crack cocaine at the age of fourteen by someone I thought I could trust.

You see the truth is I didn't realize that even though she was very kind and generous to me, she did not have my best interests at heart. You see Donna was very cunning and crafty. I never knew what she was doing because I was ignorant to the real life of adults behind closed doors. After about a month or so of hanging around Donna alone, she came up with a plan on how we could get money for food (at least that is what she said it was for). She told me that there was a man who lived up the street that she cooked for every now and then and he would pay her when she did. If I wanted to make a quick buck, he would pay me $200 just to make a meal. All I had to do was go down to his house and cook breakfast for him and he would pay me to do so. Even though I was naïve I still felt like something wasn't right with that story.

So I said, "I don't want to go down there by myself, because that is a grown man, will you go with me?" She said, "I'll go with you but first you have to look pretty. No man wants an ugly cook." So she dressed me up in a mini skirt, painted red lipstick on my lips, and finished me off in a pair of high heels. Then we walked down the alley to his house. She said, "You don't have to worry. I've known him for a long time, he's a good guy." When we got to the back door of his house she knocked on the door, and he opened it and Donna quickly walked away without saying a word.

When I walked into the kitchen to look for food, he walked over to me grabbed my hand and led me into the bedroom. I said, "what are you doing?' He said "Didn't Donna tell you why you are here?" I said "Yeah; to cook you breakfast right?" He replied, "Okay yeah, but after we're done here." He laid me on the bed and got on his knees and began performing oral sex on me. After the first attack on me and from my most recent experiences, I knew this was wrong but I never said a word. I lay there crying silently until he was done with me. Here I was again. The banner was waving, the neon sign was flashing, and the notice was on my forehead: "LOST GIRL." "NAÏVE." "THE GIRL NO ONE CARES ABOUT."

These are all the things that predators (men and women) look for when they are doing the devil's work. That's right. They are doing the devil's work. Sure they are seeking to fulfill their own wants and desires, but the devil is actually working a three-fold plot, and he is the only beneficiary in the plan. Through my abusers, and me Satan was working to satisfy his need to gain more souls into the damning kingdom of darkness. He can kill two birds with one stone by first destroying my destiny and my abuser's destiny because we all have a choice to do either God's will, or Satan's will. We are either the victims of evil, or we are the doer's of evil. It doesn't matter if it is the master or the slave. If we both continue to do things that are not in God's will, we both go to hell, and the devil wins!

When it was all over, He had the audacity to say. "That wasn't so bad was it?" He gave me the money for "cooking" then I walked into the kitchen and made him breakfast. He said to me, Donna knew what time it was. I don't know why she didn't keep it real with you. You can come and see me anytime you want without her okay?" "Okay," I replied. I now realized my "so called" big sister/pimp, just sold me to the drug dealer up the street who had to be old enough to be my father, for two hundred dollars.

After the first time it became easier. I continued going to different dealers' houses for money and sometimes drugs until one day, one guy did not want me to leave. Instead he wanted to get high with me while having intercourse. This went on all night long. I had no desire to be touched let alone have sex but that's what he required so I went along with it. I had become a slave to the enemy overnight. We were smoking freebase cocaine and having sex, to the point that I overdosed. All I really remember is being pushed out of a car at the entrance of a hospital. God must have had much mercy on me during that time because I couldn't speak to say that I needed help. But someone came for me. I had absolutely no idea how long I was overdosing before the dealer realized that I was dying. But God's grace and mercy kept me alive.

I, like my eldest brother before me, was now drinking until I blacked out. Sometimes I would wake up without knowing where I was or whom I was with. I am reminded of a guy I met by the name of Ronny when I was about 17 years old. This guy really liked me.

He would give me anything my little heart desired. Ronny was the kind of man who really knew how to treat a lady. He even knew how to treat me, just as I was, in my unstable condition. You see I was ashamed of the lifestyle that I had acquired, so I shared that part of who I was with no one. Ronny was so kind and generous to me and I knew I didn't want to lose him. The only problem with Ronny was he did not know how to say no to me.

One day, Ronny's uncle had come in from Madison to visit. I thought he was so cool. He reminded me of Frankie Beverly from Maze. That day happened to be his birthday so we partied all night long. The next morning I woke up with a massive hangover. I started looking around because I didn't recognize where I was. I peeked under the covers for Ronny, only to realize that this man was not Ronny! I was in a motel room and in the bed with his uncle! Immediately I dashed from the bed only to find that I was naked from the waist down. I was so embarrassed that I began to cry. I frantically started looking for my clothes and car keys. Disgusted with him, Ronny, and myself I screamed, "Where are my keys!" He said he didn't know. I said, "Where is my car?" He said it was at Ronny's house. So I said, "Where is Ronny?" I guess he's at home. Crying from the shame I just sat there looking at his uncle. He said nothing had happened. "If nothing happened then why am I naked?" I asked furiously. He said that I taken my clothes off but soon as I did, I passed out from the alcohol. Still to this day I don't know how true his story was. But this is what happens when an excessive amount of alcohol is in your system. Your mind and body are slaves to the chemical effects of the poisons, while the devil dances with your soul. I was an emotional wreck. I begged him to please take me to Ronny's house.

When I arrived at Ronny's I remember slapping him and telling him that it was over between us. "How could you let your uncle take me with him?" I shouted. Ronny said I was so high and out of my mind that I was behaving erratically. He said I became violent and tried to attack him, and I insisted that I was leaving with his uncle. To prevent things from escalating, he let me go. That was the last day I saw him and I would not see him again for years to come. I know my lips blamed Ronny for the way things ended.

But in my heart, I knew I had a problem and I did not know how to fix it. I started drinking more and more each day. I was secretly getting high off of crack to erase the painful memories of my youth; not knowing that this journey would cost me the next 17 years of my life.

CHAPTER EIGHT – DANCING WITH DEATH

DISCLAIMER: Please note. This part of my story graphically profiles the details my life as a call girl and a stripper (my life being the operative words.) I am in no way endorsing or glamorizing the sex trade industry in any way. The professions of this industry are risky, immoral, dangerous and mostly illegal. I am not advising or encouraging any reader to pursue a career in the sex trade industry. This was my own decision, and my experiences were a direct reflection of my own choices. I am encouraging every reader to do the opposite of what I did. I stand behind my belief that the sex trade industry is NOT purposed for God's child of destiny.

By the time I was nineteen years old I was an alcoholic, a drug addict and a call girl. Believe it or not, I would have rather had sex for money with men that I knew instead of soliciting total strangers on the streets. I knew that each way was wrong, but that was my life back then. If it was alcohol- aided, drug-driven, and sex-saturated, I was in it. I temporarily became a stripper because there was a lot of hype about how much money you could make from the job. The truth is a dancer is really not getting paid for stripping; she is getting money for prostituting herself. Basically a girl will not get as much money from dancing as she would doing the "extras" private parties, "champagne rooms" and of course the winner, sex. The twos and fews girls earned dancing, was a joke to me compared to what I was making. In fact if you made any real money, you could bet all your "tips" that being a prostitute was the way to go. I was all gung ho (no pun intended) for doing whatever, with whoever had the right price. Oh yeah, I tried it for about a year with some girlfriends of mine, only to find myself drifting, falling and eventually crashing. I was worse off than I was when I first started.

Now a few of my girlfriends were "dating" couples for money, and I found myself dating as many as three men back to back, one after another, with no regard to my own life. Yeah, it was that bad. I had a habit to support so I just wanted the money. Most of the time I was so drunk that I would pass out right there in the hotel room, right in the middle of the date. It was no one but God who kept me safe from death, sickness and disease. I have witnessed firsthand the awful calamities that plagued many other women who did the same things that I did to get money. I ran with a girl name Crystal who was one of the most beautiful women I have ever seen.

Everybody was just gaga over her. But, she fell for the wrong guy and then one day, her body was found cut in pieces, wrapped in a black garbage bag in a dumpster, behind the apartment complex where she lived.

The word on the streets was that she had gotten pregnant by her pimp and refused to get rid of the baby. So as a result, he got rid of her. He was known as what they call a guerilla pimp. Those men took women and would viciously make them work the streets. Then they would kill them at the drop of a dime for whatever reason. The incident was all a big blur to me and it just did not seem real. I remember sobbing in the dressing room with the other girls trying to figure out what had happened. I tried so many different drugs in those forthcoming months. It is a wonder that I am here today to tell my testimony with a sane mind. I often think back on some of the scariest moments of my life as a stripper/ prostitute, and I give God all the glory for sparing me to tell my story. These painful recollections are being recanted in an effort to save someone else's life. I know there is a confused little girl, a lonely teenager, and some troubled women who are going through the same things that I went through in one aspect or another and I pray that they seek God for direction concerning it all. I find myself reflecting on the moment when the first woman I attached myself to, prostituted me. Not long after that, I was prostituting myself. The cycle had come full circle, and it was full blown. All of the people that I trusted led me down a path of danger, destruction and death.

Sometimes I thought, what is wrong with those people? What kind of life is this? This was not living! Do they even care about themselves? Until the realization kicked in that I too was now one of these people.

One thing I did learn though is that most people, who ended up in these predicaments, were usually victims themselves. Someone showed them a life of sin, or they were abused in some way, so the cycle continued on. The only difference was that I did not desire to hurt anyone, and I knew in order for me to stay alive, my life had to change.

While stripping I met men who were known as "sugar daddies." These older men were the type of men who would buy me nice things, take me to beautiful places and load my pockets with cash. Some of them would even supply my drug habit just to be in my presence. It had gotten to the point where a couple of them had gotten really strung out and went broke chasing after my habit and me. Most of them were very old Caucasian men whom I treated very badly. I was ashamed to go anywhere with them in the public so I would make them sit in the car while I did whatever I was going to do. A couple of them were younger white men who did not look so bad, but they had strange fetishes.

For instance there was one who would request for me to urinate on him, and as much as I loved the money and attention he gave me, his "fantasy" was a filthy and complete turn-off! I could not get past the fact that this man loved to be drenched in urine and then would want to lie next to me! No amount of money was worth that disgust and humiliation! Then another one would want to sit and smoke crack all day and night, no sex just high. Sure he gave me a lot of money but consequentially, his habit was fierce compared to mine! He would load himself with so much dope that he would begin to think that I was out to hurt him, which always made me question, if he was going to hurt me. I did not stick around long enough to find out.

I met a girl named Dawn. She was like a book, just smart, pretty, funny and rich. When I say rich, I mean rich! She was so rich that no one worked in her family. They did two main things with money. They managed it and spent it all day. Dawn was the type of person who was always straight up, forward and to the point. With her, what you saw is what you got.

She would always say she knew she would die young. She would often tell me that I should start living life because tomorrow wasn't promised. I hated when she would talk like that. It would just spook me out. I tried taking her advice so I walked away from the life of a stripper, but I could not walk away from the drugs. So I kept the regulars that I met to supply my habits and to take care of my necessities.

I even moved in with one of my sugar daddies, which happened to live in a small town up north in Beaver Dam, WI. At that time, there were absolutely no black people living there, so I was like a fish out of water, demographically. I didn't even trust this guy; I just didn't have anywhere else to go. For added security and familiarity, I brought my mom and my brother to move in with me. I was afraid of living there alone with him. We had absolutely nothing in common except for the fact that I needed money and a place to stay and he had both. I lived in that house for nine years and for nine years, he supplied my drug and alcohol habits, and carried the weight of my mom my brother and myself. The time seemed like it was one long year instead of nine. My life was so redundant that every day seemed to be the same as yesterday.

There were times that I would travel out of town. I took my own supply of drugs with me or I would find them while I was out. I used to go visit my girlfriends in Milwaukee. One of the girls I ran with, Theresa had landed herself in a pimp/ whore relationship. She was being pimped by this guy whom she loved like no other. No one, especially me understood her reasons. It was probably because of his good looks. He was a carmel colored man with the most beautiful grey eyes, silky black wavy hair and a pretty decent physique. She would often say it was the sex but either way, she wasn't going anywhere. She was relentlessly in love with him and she would do whatever he told her to do. I remember he sent her to Hawaii for about two months straight, she doing it all I'm sure. When she returned she had apparently made thousands of dollars that he dumped out on the table in front of me, in hopes that it would sway me to join them in their boisterous debauchery. He walked out of the house leaving her a bag of cocaine to get high with. Immediately she turned to me and asked if I could give her ten dollars! I couldn't believe that he never gave her a dime, just dope, clothes and jewelry. I would think this to myself and sometimes ask her, "what was the purpose of being with him? Her reply would always be the same. "Olivia you don't understand!" I would say, "Theresa, you're right I don't!"

Then there was Vesta, every time I would see her, she was pregnant, again and again! I did not get it. She tried dancing but mostly she was the type of woman who was in love with the idea of being loved by some big time drug dealer or pimp. She would lie, steal, cheat, and do whatever she could to get her claws into these men and many times she did. I stopped hanging out with her so much once we were over twenty-one because I found her to be very shady in our friendship. I could not trust her. She would steal from me and then brag to people about how she did it. Once she stole my gold herringbone necklace from my house, I cut her off.

Then there was Sandy. Sandy was the friend whom I called my cousin because we grew up together. Our parents also grew up together, and her uncle and my aunt hooked up and had a child so we were really close. I actually took Sandy out of town with me one weekend and introduced her to the dance scene. Sandy wasn't the smartest girl and she could barely read or write. But somehow, she was really good at making and managing money. She was a good example of "using what you have to get what you want." The girl knew how to entertain and from the time she auditioned, got hired and started her first gig, she was on fire! She acquired professional management to get her booked at some of the top clubs, in and out of the country. She found her niche in dancing, then dating and sure enough like my drugs, she was hooked. She just could not let it go. I heard that while she was on the island of Guam, someone "laced" her with something and she temporarily lost her mind. But once she recovered, she was right back in rotation.

CHAPTER NINE – ALIVE BUT NOT LIVING

By the time I was twenty-five I was so tired of getting high that I used to pray to God and ask Him to let me die. Can you believe that? The girl who had so many hopes for singing for God, who was once so full of life, and dreamed of a prospective future, was now pleading for God to end her life! It seemed that I had nothing left to live for because my life was nothing but one big drug induced cloud. I would say, "Please God let this be the last time. I just want to overdose and die tonight." So I would buy a lot of dope and try to use it all in one setting. I often did it with the expectant hope that I would die. But God blocked it every time! He wouldn't let it be so! I used to think, why wouldn't God let me die? I know I am not fit to live. I hated the fact that I did not know love. I did not know how to love. I did not even love myself. I was so withdrawn from the world, mostly because I struggled with my identity and was so insecure and unsure of whom I was.

Then one day I met a young lady by the name of Nikki through a mutual acquaintance, and from the moment I said hello to her, she began making plans to leave with me. She kept saying, "I want to be your friend and not in that way. I have to go with you. I don't know why, but I know I'm supposed to go with you", she would say. Now as strange as it may sound, I actually let her go with me that day we met, along with our mutual acquaintance, Princess. Well unbeknownst to me, this young lady would play a vital part in my life, in regards to my relationship with God. Who would have thought?

You see God had a plan for my life that I was completely oblivious to. I was walking into my house with Nikki and Princess that night, and Nikki, who was a lot younger than I was, (I was twenty-five at the time and Nikki was a mere eighteen,) seemed very mature. She walked over to a bookshelf in the house. There was a Bible sitting on it covered in dust. She picked it up, blew the dust off the top of it, and opened it to Psalm 23. She then told me to read it. Ok really?

I already had a weird feeling about her but now I wasn't feeling her at all! She wasn't in the house for two minutes and already she aggravated me! I thought to myself. Due to my drug habit, I had gotten so far away from God. I barely prayed. In fact my only prayer was to ask God to save me or allow me to die; so surely I was not reading His word. I got upset with her and said, "No!" She said, "Yeah, I don't know why but you are supposed to learn this prayer; It's yours, she said".

I stared at her for a moment then a feeling of utter fear had come over me. I thought to myself I must be in some real trouble with God for Him to send someone to the earth for me. I know that may sound strange to the average person, but I tell you that is exactly how I felt. Honestly I couldn't tell you the last time I had read anything in the Bible, so it all seemed to be foreign to me. She said, "Here, let me help you", as she began reading along with me.

"The Lord is my shepherd I shall not want. He makes me lie down in green pastures. He leads me beside the still waters. He restores my soul. He leads me in the path of righteousness for His name's sake. Yea though I walk through the valley of the shadow of death I will fear no evil for Thou are with me. Thy rod and Thy staff they comfort me. Thou prepares a table before me in the presence of my enemies. Thou anoint my head with oil, my cup runs over. Surely goodness and mercy shall follow me all the days of my life and I will dwell in the house of the Lord forever." -Psalm 23 Amen!

There was awkwardness in the room. Just when I was about to go and get high, we start reading the Bible? What was that all about? Then she says to me out of nowhere, "I'm going to be there." Completely baffled, I asked, "Be there? Where? When what happens? When it happens to you?

WHEN WHAT HAPPENS?" At this point she was making me completely uncomfortable. I said, "Be where? When what happens to me Nikki?" I said it in a tone that seemed to state, "You better tell me something!" Princess then looked at me and said, "What are you talking about Nikki?" "You're the one talking!" Nikki replied. Princess and I looked at each other puzzled. It seemed as if Nikki had no memory of what she just said. I was upset so I walked upstairs.

Upstairs is where I went to get high and I did not want them in the room because I never wanted to be the reason anyone would start using drugs, and I would do my best to discourage them; especially the youth. I hated the habit that I had acquired and I never forgot how it all began in my life. I felt that I would get in trouble with God if I ever turned anyone on to drugs, especially a kid! I vowed that as long as Nikki stayed with me, she would never see me use.

That first night was crazy! I had bought an Ouija Board from local toy store earlier that week, but never had anyone to play it with. I wasn't even sure if what people said about was true. Plus it was in the toy store, so how harmful could it really be? I thought. So I bought one. I asked the girls to play with me. So we sat at the dining room table and began asking it questions and just like that, the glass piece began to move and spell out words. It told us that Princess did not like Nikki and that they were going to have a fight. Princess quickly became enraged and she stood up and slapped Nikki! Just like that it was on. Before I could say anything they were fighting. I was completely caught off guard, never expecting anything like that to happen - especially right after the board's eerie prediction! I grabbed the girls and pulled them apart. Blood was everywhere! I looked to see where the blood was coming from and I noticed that Princess had bitten a chunk of meat off of Nikki's face! "Princess!" I shouted. You have to go! "Why me," she asked? "Because you started it!" I yelled! Holding her, I grabbed my car keys and walked Princess to the car leaving Nikki in the house. "I'll be right back, I'm so sorry." I felt awful that all this happened in my house. Princess screamed at the top of her lungs, "She's the devil"! Get her out of your house!" I did not know what to do. I just knew Princess's behavior was way over the top and she if anyone had to go.

After everything died down that night all I could think about was how quickly the madness ensued. I felt guilty because it was my house and my Ouija board. I had no idea what was about to happen in my life considering that I did not even know who this person (Nikki) was in my house! Yet I felt like she had to stay with me, at least until her face healed. So I patched her up then sat and talked with her, trying to feel her out, in an attempt to get to know her better. I asked her questions like where was she from, if she have any kids, how she met Princess etc; we seemed to get along pretty well. I agreed to let her stay for a few months. Even though Princess said some pretty messed up stuff about Nikki, the truth was if the devil was in anybody it was Princess. I believe that Satan recognized that God was using Nikki to reveal his plan to me, so he tried desperately to stop that from taking place. For those of you who do not know, I am here to tell you that POWER belongs to GOD! Although it was a strange way to get my attention, He got it!

Complete deliverance doesn't all happen overnight but this event signaled the start of it. I tell you truth Nikki would not let up on me about learning that prayer. I would act like I could not memorize it because it was too long, but she was not giving up that easy. Every now and then she would say, "Say your prayer. Let's see if you got it." I would try just to shut her up and keep it moving

I wanted to talk to the Ouija board again, but Nikki refused to touch it after what happened to her the first time. So I had another girl play with me.

She kept insisting that the Ouija was nothing to play with, but I would just act as if I did not hear her. The spirit in the board was cunning to say the least. It offered to give me everything I ever wanted in exchange for my soul. It said things to me that I knew would make me happy so I began to consider asking it one evening, (the fact that I would even consider consulting the board showed how disconnected I was from God) "Will I ever sing again?" Due to all the drug use I could no longer sing and I knew that it would mean the world to me to be able to sing again.

The board response was yes, then it begin to spell out how it would make my name great and I would be respected in many homes. It even promised to give me long flowing hair, which was one thing I thought would make me beautiful, silly me. I did not like the fact that my hair was always so short and thick. Just when I had made up mind to give in, there was a knock on the door.

There stood a Caucasian man smiling and waving. There was a bright light in the distance so I could not make out his face clearly enough to recognize him, but I opened the door anyway. He walked in, and went directly to the table where the Ouija board sat. He grabbed the board and broke it into four pieces he then walked to the counter where there was a bottle of lighter fluid and a lighter. He grabbed a metal trashcan from the hall and said, "Come with me to send this spirit off." The whole time I'm screaming, "Who are you and what are you doing?" I noticed the young lady I was plying it with was scared but she was helping him with his request for the things he needed. Then he walked outside and he placed the Ouija pieces in the trashcan. He doused lighter fluid on top on the board pieces, and set it on fire. The man looked at me and told me to say good-bye, and speak well over the spirit that we were freeing. With tears in my eyes I begin to say things like, "I hope you find your way out of darkness and I'm sorry, but I have to let you go." The flames were as tall as I was and were roaring. The man said a prayer over the fire, and we watched the fire slowly die out.

There was a release that had come over me. I said to the man, "Who are you?" He replied, "David." That night he stayed around just hanging out. He even went to the bar with us but he did not drink. He was a very gentle man with big hazel eyes and blond hair; he stood about 5'11 in height. I will never forget him. He left some time in the night and I never seen or heard from him again. To this day, I believe he was an angel sent from heaven to save me from selling my soul.

CHAPTER TEN – I AM… IN THE BUILDING

A couple of days later Nikki came to the house with drugs of her own. I could smell them. I asked her where she got them from and she said she bought them. She had been staying with me for over a month or so now and I never knew she got high because when I was upstairs, she was downstairs, and we were both doing the same thing at the same time. I was stricken with guilt over this, and I blamed myself. However, Nikki insisted that she had been using for a while and I had nothing to do with it. Soon after, we were getting high together.

Through this incident, I learned that darkness couldn't lead darkness into the light. Only light can cast out the dark. My dark influence overshadowed the little light that she had left I thought. I really had a hard time dealing with that, but I know that God sent her to me I didn't know that then but I know now. As I stated earlier, we all have a choice to do the will of God. I am not saying that Nikki is not God's child; I know that He was using her in the earth. She just made her choice. She chose to let drugs dim her light just as I had.

A couple of weeks later she came to me and ask if I would take her out of town to dance. As I had mentioned earlier dancers (strippers) were just undercover prostitutes that worked the clubs and I was not about to turn her out knowing the outcome will never be what she thought it would be. She kept insisting that if I did not take her, she would go with this guy she'd met in Madison. I knew that if I did not take her she would be pimped by that guy. Against everything I believed in, I schooled her on how to talk, walk and how to get money. I even changed her name because you become a different person when you choose to live that lifestyle. Her name was now Chyna. I even took Chyna out for her first audition. She made good tips and she received plenty of phone numbers, which is how it all begins.

When we returned home that evening, she gave all the money she made to me. I was not prepared for that and frankly, I did not like it. I was not a madam, pimp or anything else for that matter. Quickly she began dating different men and bringing the money back to me too. After a couple of times I stopped taking money from her and I told her to keep what she made to buy things that she needed for herself. If "tricking" was going to be her recreation of choice, I did not want anything to do with it. The money was not mine to keep anyway and it made me uncomfortable because it reminded me of Donna. It was like history repeating itself except this time; I was the adult with the drug habit prostituting a teenager. I could not do it, my heart would not let me and I was not cut out for that.

Now this day was the day of all days to say the least. Chyna wanted to go to Madison to audition at a club that had a big reputation for wealthy men and big money. This day would prove to be the greatest day of my life. I drove Chyna to Madison from Beaver Dam, which is about a 45-minute drive. The drive was odd and strange. It was as if I saw nothing along the way. No signs or vehicles; nothing. When we arrived to the club, the owner wanted both of us to try out. I had no plans on auditioning but it felt like it was something I was supposed to do. The men in the club bought us drinks as soon as we entered the place. I decided to audition because the crowd was so friendly which was very unusual. Between the two of us we had over three hundred dollars from a two-song audition, which again was way out of the ordinary. Chyna said, "Let's go to Milwaukee." I responded, "Are you sure? Let's go get some stuff." We hopped in the car and off to Milwaukee we went. We couldn't believe how everything just seemed to be working in our favor but it was and that wasn't the end of it.

We arrived in Milwaukee a little before midnight. I remember because we wanted to get something to drink and we were looking to find a bootlegger. Chyna said, "Let's get a room and just stay over night in Milwaukee instead of going back to Beaver Dam". "That's cool," I said. So we pulled into the driveway of the Diamond Inn motel. This motel was where everybody went to do his or her dirt. They never complained about anything that was going on in the rooms as long as you paid your bill. So I said, "Okay Chyna you go in and get the room, I don't have my I.D." Chyna hesitated, "No you go or come in with me. I'm scared." "Scared of what girl?" Shaking my head I got out of the car and said, "Just come on."

We walked in and the man at the desk was a new guy. I mean I had never seen him before and I knew all of them because I was a regular at the Diamond Inn. I asked, "Are you new here?" He said, "I AM" and just like that he slid a room key across the front desk. I just looked at it. "Here you go." He said. Still in disbelief, I say, "Ok, don't you want to see my I.D"? He smiled and said, "No, you're alright!" Laughing but not really I said, "Well, here is the $50.00 for the room?" he said, "No, it's on me." "It's on you?" I said, "you're not coming in our room with us, it's not that kind of party". He said, "I never said that." Looking at the key I glanced over at Chyna like, "what do you think?" She said, "Just get it!" Again I said, "Well, what's wrong with the room it must be crappy?" He said "No, actually its one of our best rooms." So I took the key and as we were walking up the back hallway behind the building, we were looking around to see if anyone was following us. Once we made it into the room, we examined it to find that it actually was one of the best rooms I had ever seen in all my visits there! All I could think about was we got an extra $50.00 to party with! I know right?

Chyna said, "If you want me to, I will go get the party favors and the drinks and you could chill here." I told her, "Well I don't want to be here by myself too long so hurry up because I still don't know about that front desk man." She agreed to go and come right back, so anxiously I sat and waited.

CHAPTER ELEVEN – ANGELS ON TELEVISION

As I sat and waited I could sense a strong presence in the room. I was not sure of what it was, but it really made me antsy. I began pacing the floor. I called for Chyna on the phone but she did not answer. I was so nervous and really wasn't sure why, but I could not stop my heart from beating out of my chest. I wasn't high on anything I thought, so why was I being so paranoid? An hour had passed and still, no Chyna. Now, I am beginning to worry. Where could she be I thought? To try and pass the time, I turned the TV. on but I kept the volume low enough just in case I heard something. I didn't need any surprises at this point. Before I knew it, it was 2 o'clock in the morning.

Now, I am feeling really nervous because I can't seem to shake this feeling and now growing stronger by the minute. I wanted to connect the feeling to Chyna's absence, but something was telling me that it was not it. Then out of nowhere, the T.V. began playing Mahalia Jackson's songs back-to- back and loud. As I sat on the bed I looked up to the television thinking, why is that so loud? I noticed the commercial seemed to last forever As it ended there was a voice which said, "THERE WILL NEVER BE ANOTHER MAHALIA JACKSON" as if it was talking directly to me.

As I mentioned earlier, I always carried with me the dream of singing like the great Mahalia Jackson. There was something special about her that I saw in myself. I used to think that she was a real live angel. So I took the commercial personal. I began to cry, I felt like I had really messed things up and having any chance of ever harnessing greatness like that of the incomparable Mahalia Jackson. Redemption is not possible for people like me I thought. My life was riddled with sin, shame, guilt and defeat. How could God ever consider me let alone giving me my voice back after all the years I wasted? How could He; Mahailia was a holy, sanctified, spirit filled woman, I was just the opposite…

I sat there sobbing on the bed begging God to SAVE ME because I did not want to die in the state that I was in. I begin to saying in my heart, I'm sorry for disappointing you God, please hear me. I knew if God would come for me and rescue me from this dead place that I could live and maybe even sing like the great Mahalia. Then again, the same commercial repeated just as loud, but this time something was different about the voice at the end. It said, "There will never be another Mahalia Jackson" as to say (there can't be another Mahalia) but there can be YOU! Something inside me leaped. All of a sudden, I felt like there was hope for me.

This time the voice was comforting. Though I know it was the same commercial because every song stood out. There were songs I had never heard before but it was all Mahalia and it was all God. I looked up in anticipation, waiting on God, and then I heard a voice say… "HERE I COME!" Suddenly, there was a knock at the door. No it wasn't Jesus, it was Chyna. There she stood with two men, with drinks in one hand, and bags of dope in the other. Quickly I pushed the men back and said, "You can't come in here!" Slamming the door behind them, I grabbed Chyna and said in a frantic voice, "GOD IS COMING!" Without hesitation we both scurried to the bed and under the covers we went peeking out with expectation.

Then it happened, the visitation I was longing for. THE LORD JESUS WAS IN THE ROOM. I remember Chyna saying, "Say thank you Jesus, say thank you Jesus." I said it over and over, "Thank you Jesus, thank you Jesus, thank you Jesus," but to no avail. I could hear the spirit asking me, "Why are you thanking me?" "I don't know," I exclaimed. Again He would ask, "Why are you thanking me?" "I don't know!" Trying with all my might to get up but could not. It was as if I was being held down. I remember being stretched out on the floor like Jesus was on the cross. I continued to say "thank you Jesus" but the spirit would say, "why are you thanking me?" I began to cry because I truly had no idea why I was thanking Him and most of all He knew that.

Then like an instant replay video I saw flashes of my life before my eyes. (No, I wasn't dying; I was being made new). I saw every moment of danger that I escaped from. When I was spared from the school bus accident He said, "That was me who spared you from death." I was in the second grade when that happened, and had completely forgotten about that. Again, one episode after another was flashing and I could hear the spirit saying, "That was me" after each scene. I said "Thank you Jesus!" with a heart of gratitude.

As I lay there on the floor I began to sob because I realized that God has been with me my entire life, and I could not imagine what He was thinking as I saturated myself with the drugs and alcohol, and all of the men I laid with for money. Oh the shame that had come over me! I could remember every scene even though I had not thought about them in years. I realized the magnitude of the many reasons I had to be thankful and I AM! So many times God rescued me and protected me and I didn't even know it. Slowly my limbs begin to move, I began to thank Him with my whole heart with all sincerity. Now, I was on my feet and He stretched out His hand and said to me, "Take hold of my hand and I will guide you back to me. Timidly, I reached up so afraid, that I would stumble or fall. I nervously grabbed a hold of His hand saying to Him "I'm scared. The Lord spoke to me and said, "DO NOT BE AFRAID FOR I AM WITH YOU"... and there I was walking with the

Lord. Me, walking with the Lord! I began to feel like I was the most important person in the world at the luckiest. God said to me that He would lead me back to Him and all I had to do was trust and follow Him.

The whole experience went on for hours. It would take another book to tell you about it all, but just know from that day my life would never be the same. I looked up and there stood Mahalia Jackson smiling. The spirit said "sing your prayer." With a little skepticism unsure if I could, I opened my mouth and I began to sing the prayer of Psalm 23 in its entirety, with the voice of the great Mahalia Jackson. To my amazement, it was absolutely beautiful. The last thing I heard was a voice saying; "NOW GO TELL THE WORLD THAT YOU HAVE BEEN SAVED" So, I grabbed what I could (without even considering what I might look like after such an encounter with the Lord); and said to Chyna, "Let's go! "I've got to tell the world that I've been saved." We got out of there so fast, leaving everything behind. To God be the glory I Am saved!

From that moment on I have always been conscious about God and His presence, about what's right or wrong and what's good or bad. I know God is real and He is watching over me like He's watching over you. To this day, Psalm 23 is my prayer…I take it personally. God walks with me and I walk with Him.

CHAPTER TWELVE – LIFE AFTER THE RUSH

Transforming a lifestyle of sin into a lifestyle of holiness is a learned behavior. It did not happen at once although I wish it did. I had my share of pitfalls and setbacks but I knew the path to Christ was the right path for my life and will always be so I continued to get back up and try again. I had moments where the devil would bring back things of my past to make me think I was missing something. I even had times where I felt all alone but I would remember the WORD of God; He promised to never leave me or forsake me Hebrews 13:5 I had to carry certain affirmation scriptures with me daily to overcome the enemy for instance (Thy word I have hid in my heart that I may not sin against Thee…Psalm 119:11). It would remind me how much more important it was to me to please God than it was to please myself. Serving God is a sure thing. This path leads to true happiness, peace, joy, love and so much more. I now live a life worth living. I abide in Christ and He abides in me (John 15:4) and through Him I have conquered the odds.

A SPECIAL MESSAGE FOR THE YOUTH~ I know life doesn't always deal out the best hand, and we wish we could even trade in our life for a new one, but it just doesn't happen like that. It can even get to the point where we feel like no one understands us. We think we're all alone and we have no one to turn to. But God… let me reassure you, that there is someone who cares. Someone who is concerned about what you are concerned about.

The Bible says in Psalm 138:8 that the "Lord will perfect that which concerns me"(you) your Father knows what you need before you ask of Him." (Matthew 6:8). Seek and you shall find, believe that because it's true. "Trust in the Lord with all your heart and lean not unto your own understanding, in all your ways acknowledge Him in all your ways and He shall direct your path." (Proverbs 3;5). "Even now you can begin to seek the Lord, don't let the excitement of youth cause you to forget your Creator. Honor Him in your youth before you grow old and say life isn't pleasant anymore." (Ecclesiastes 12:1).

Life is worth living as a pre-teen, teen-ager or adult. Wherever you are at this period of your life, ENJOY IT! You can begin to make choices for yourself concerning which way you will grow and go. Your physical appearance will change, and your mental state will be challenged by many influences, but your spiritual state will determine which path you will follow. In those times when no one understands, it is crucial that you find your balance in your life.

You may find yourself working in the kingdom of God or working in the kingdom of darkness. It is your life, so please be wise when you make your choice. Instead of being a victim of circumstance, take responsibility for your actions and grow up trained. The Bible says in (Proverbs 22:6) "Train up a child in the way he should go and when (she) is old (she) will not depart from it." Even if you notice no one is being responsible over your soul, you take charge! In Romans 10:14 it reads, "How then can they call on Him in whom they have not believed? And how can they believe in Him of whom they have not heard? And how can they hear without a preacher?" Pray and ask God to lead you to a good Bible teaching church so you can learn more about Him and how to serve Him.

Healthy Tips:

1. Obey your parents and those who are given authority over you.

2. Spend quality time with God (He will guard your heart and mind).

3. Stay within your age group (within 2 years either way).

4. Trust your instincts (if it doesn't feel right it probably isn't).

5. Value yourself (material things can never compare to what you are worth).

6. Educate yourself (knowledge is power…good or bad).

7. Preserve yourself (marriage is worth the wait).

8. Practice virtues (self-discipline, moral excellence, goodness, righteousness, compassion, courage, loyalty, responsibility, faith, honesty etc.).

9. Think on these things, whatever is true, noble, right, pure, lovely, honest, praiseworthy, and things that are excellent!

10. Last but not least know that God is always with you even until the end of time.

God saved me from a life of death and destruction so I could share my story with you. A story of a little girl trapped in big a world; that somehow found herself in a hurry to grow up; only to find that she was headed nowhere and fast. You see destruction discriminates against no one. It can plague the rich, the poor, the young and the old, any race, creed and gender; you name it. Destruction seeks to find itself in the people of God. The enemies plan is, the sooner destruction finds you the quicker it'll destroy you.

It is only by God's grace that I am here today. I stand as a woman who has overcome the snares of this world; but only through faith, perseverance, self- love and most of all the help of the Lord. I had to learn, yes, the hard way, but you do not have to. I had to allow Jesus to come into my life to give me direction. (to come means: to move toward something; approach; to move or journey to vicinity with a specified purpose). It is a small word but it has such a profound meaning. We are all connected to this small word. I remember a young wise man once told me, "We come into this world to overcome the many obstacles to become who God has called us to be" and I concur.

God will call you, and when He calls you to walk in His will, which is His plan for your life; He already knows what your future entails. "For I know the plans I have for you, declares the LORD, plans to prosper you and not to harm you, plans to give you hope and an expected end." – Jeremiah 29:11

Please do not resist God He truly has your best interests at heart. And understand that He does not have to call, nor does He have to repeat Himself. "For many are called, but few are chosen." – Matthew 22:14 take full advantage of the call.

ENJOY YOUR YOUTH. God will eventually bring you to adulthood, gradually, and ON TIME. When you move too fast, you stall your present life with your future problems. For instance, a girl can give up everything she is supposed to experience in her youth if she has a baby too young. She misses high school, prom, and college etc. all for the wrong reasons. The birth of a child comes from a relationship designed by God, which is marriage. Because of adult behavior in one's adolescent years a future has been stalled! By moving out of season, you gain the future without graduating from your present. You become stunted and stagnated, which eventually will fill you with resentment. Do not resent your life! Enjoy it!

I have been richly and unfathomably blessed, all because I chose to walk in God's light. I chose life; I did not choose any life, I chose new life, the life God wanted me to have. This is the life that He promised me now, at the right age. My mind is mature enough to handle what He has given me. My body betrayed my mind back in those days. Or better yet, my body looked the part, but my mind LACKED the requirements needed to be an adult.

That is why so many of those people were able to take advantage of me. My mind was still that of a child, but I was playing adult games with a child like mentality. THIS DOES NOT HAVE TO BE YOU...DON'T RUSH TO GET OLD!

I'd like to share with you an update on what the young ladies I ran with are doing today.

To my disappointment, and in fulfillment of her premonition of dying at an early age, Dawn died of an overdose at the age of 25.

Vesta has 7 children by 7 different men and never married.

Theresa had a stroke and is now paralyzed on her left side from her head to her toe and is still using street drugs.

Sandy is currently a 40-year-old stripper with 2 children and a pimp.

Chyna went on to become a cracked out porn star in Beverly Hills, CA.

Yet there is a God who cares for them all, and there is absolutely nothing too hard for Him, so my prayer is this, God if you did it for me surly you can do it for them…SAVE THEM and be a blessing to their children and their children's children. In Jesus name, Amen!

I want to say that God is and always will be the center of my life. The day I said yes to God was the day I chose life. After I made that decision, my life has never been the same. I have overcome many obstacles in His name and continue to make progress. I want to hear God say… well done thy good and faithful servant. Truly I am a grateful woman. I have witnessed God not only hear but answer my prayers since that unbelievable encounter.

God allows me to use a voice to minister in song and I take nothing He gives me for granted, He has opened up a creative side of me that I never knew existed. And to top it all off He gives me the pleasure of serving Him.

There's nothing I'd rather do!

Currently, I am a minister of the gospel, touring across the country ministering God's word in song. I also participate in public speaking engagements, sharing my testimony with ladies of all ages, encouraging them to move forward in what God has called them to be. I also have had the opportunity to record and write my own original songs. TO GOD BE THE GLORY!

Last but certainly not least, I praise God for my wonderful family. I finally have the family that I have always desired. Along with Jesus, my family is the center of my joy! God has kept His word, and His promise of restoration to me and I have so much to be thankful for and cannot imagine my life without Him. Praise God for deliverance, and from whom all blessings flow!

Some names of individuals have been changed to protect the identity and privacy of the innocent.

Time for Everything: Ecclesiastes 3:1-8

1 There is a time for everything, and a season for every activity under heaven:

2a time to be born and a time to die, a time to plant and a time to uproot, 3a time to kill and a time to heal, a time to tear down and a time to build,

4a time to weep and a time to laugh, a time to mourn and a time to dance,

5a time to scatter stones and a time to gather them, a time to embrace and a time to refrain,

6a time to search and a time to give up, a time to keep and a time to throw away, 7a time to tear and a time to mend, a time to be silent and a time to speak,

8a time to love and a time to hate, a time for war and a time for peace.

Printed in the United States
By Bookmasters